Dear Parents and Educators,

Welcome to Penguin Young Readers! As parents and educators, you know that each child develops at his or her own pace—in terms of speech, critical thinking, and, of course, reading. Penguin Young Readers recognizes this fact. As a result, each Penguin Young Readers book is assigned a traditional easy-to-read level (1–4) as well as a Guided Reading Level (A–P). Both of these systems will help you choose the right book for your child. Please refer to the back of each book for specific leveling information. Penguin Young Readers features esteemed authors and illustrators, stories about favorite characters, fascinating nonfiction, and more!

Nina, Nina Star Ballerina

LEVEL **2**

GUIDED READING LEVEL **G**

This book is perfect for a **Progressing Reader** who:
• can figure out unknown words by using picture and context clues;
• can recognize beginning, middle, and ending sounds;
• can make and confirm predictions about what will happen in the text; and
• can distinguish between fiction and nonfiction.

Here are some **activities** you can do during and after reading this book:
• Vocabulary: In this story, there is a misunderstanding between Nina and her friend Ann about the word *star*. Discuss with the child the different meanings of the word.
• Character Traits: Nina is an interesting character. Write down some traits that describe her.

Remember, sharing the love of reading with a child is the best gift you can give!

—Bonnie Bader, EdM
  Penguin Young Readers program

*Penguin Young Readers are leveled by independent reviewers applying the standards developed by Irene Fountas and Gay Su Pinnell in *Matching Books to Readers: Using Leveled Books in Guided Reading*, Heinemann, 1999.

For my star of a mom—JOC

To ballerinas everywhere—DD

Penguin Young Readers
Published by the Penguin Group
Penguin Group (USA) Inc., 375 Hudson Street, New York, New York 10014, USA
Penguin Group (Canada), 90 Eglinton Avenue East, Suite 700, Toronto, Ontario M4P 2Y3, Canada
(a division of Pearson Penguin Canada Inc.)
Penguin Books Ltd, 80 Strand, London WC2R 0RL, England
Penguin Ireland, 25 St Stephen's Green, Dublin 2, Ireland (a division of Penguin Books Ltd)
Penguin Group (Australia), 707 Collins Street, Melbourne, Victoria 3008, Australia
(a division of Pearson Australia Group Pty Ltd)
Penguin Books India Pvt Ltd, 11 Community Centre, Panchsheel Park, New Delhi–110 017, India
Penguin Group (NZ), 67 Apollo Drive, Rosedale, Auckland 0632, New Zealand
(a division of Pearson New Zealand Ltd)
Penguin Books (South Africa), Rosebank Office Park,
181 Jan Smuts Avenue, Parktown North 2193, South Africa
Penguin China, B7 Jiaming Center, 27 East Third Ring Road North,
Chaoyang District, Beijing 100020, China

Penguin Books Ltd, Registered Offices: 80 Strand, London WC2R 0RL, England

Text copyright © 1997 by Jane O'Connor. Illustrations © 1997 by DyAnne DiSalvo. All rights reserved. First published in 1997 by Grosset & Dunlap, an imprint of Penguin Group (USA) Inc. Published in 2013 by Penguin Young Readers, an imprint of Penguin Group (USA) Inc., 345 Hudson Street, New York, New York 10014. Manufactured in China.

Library of Congress Control Number: 96030741

ISBN 978-0-448-41492-8

10 9 8 7 6 5 4 3 2 1

Nina, Nina Star Ballerina

by Jane O'Connor
illustrated by DyAnne DiSalvo

Penguin Young Readers
An Imprint of Penguin Group (USA) Inc.

Dance class is over.

Nina runs out to Mom.

"Hooray!" Nina shouts.

"There is going

to be a dance show.

Our dance is called

Night Sky."

Mom and Nina drive home.

"Eric is the moon,"

Nina tells Mom.

"The rest of us are stars.

We twinkle around him."

That night

Mom and Nina look

at pictures in the album.

There is Nina the butterfly

and Nina the elf.

"Soon we can put in

new pictures,"

says Mom.

"Pictures of my little star."

The next day at lunch

Nina sits next to Ann.

Nina likes Ann best

of all the girls.

She tells Ann

about the dance show.

"I am a star," Nina says.

"That is so great!"

says Ann.

Then she pokes

Beth and Emily.

"Guess what?" says Ann.

"Nina is in a dance show.

And she is the star!"

"Cool!" says Beth.

"Wow!" says Emily.

"The star!

You must be so good."

Nina does not know

what to say.

She is **a** star.

She is not **the** star.

But all the fuss is nice.

So Nina eats her hot dog.

She does not say a thing.

At the next dance class

Nina watches Miss Dawn.

"Point your hands.

Point your feet.

Be pointy like a star,"

Miss Dawn tells the girls.

"Then spin and twinkle

around Eric

the moon."

Nina learns
all the steps.

But sometimes
her feet will not do
what she wants.
And spinning is hard.

"Better,"
says Miss Dawn.

But Miss Dawn

never says "Great"

like she says

to some kids.

Nina is glad
Ann cannot see her.

On Saturday

Ann comes over to play.

They hide out in a cave.

The cave is made of sheets.

It is cold in the cave.

But they must hide

from the bear.

"Grandma called,"

Mom tells Nina.

"She can't come

to the dance show."

Ann looks at Nina.

"Nina, could I come?

I would love to see

you dance."

"NO!" thinks Nina.

"Yes," says Mom.

"Of course you may come."

Now what will Nina do?

That night Nina cannot sleep.

The show is in three days!

Ann will find out

Nina is not a real star.

Maybe Ann will not like her

anymore.

The next day

Nina has a plan.

It is not a good plan.

But it is the only plan

she can think of.

All day she limps

around the house.

She limps at the supermarket

and at the pizza place.

"My leg hurts,"

Nina keeps saying.

Nina does not look at Mom

when she says this.

She does not like to fib.

That night Nina takes a bath.

"My leg still hurts," she says.

"Maybe I can't be

in the dance show!"

Mom looks at Nina.

"Do you **want** to be in it?"

"Yes!" says Nina.

But then she starts to cry.

Nina tells Mom everything.

Mom tells Nina to tell Ann.

"Ann will understand,"

says Mom.

Nina is not so sure.

At school Nina sees Ann.

"Ann, I have something
to tell you.

I am not **the** star of the show.

Three other kids are stars, too.

It is no big deal."

Ann shrugs.

"So what?

I just want to see you dance."

Then she gives Nina a locket.

It looks like a star.

"I hope you like this.

It shines in the dark."

It is the day

of the dance show.

Mom and Ann are there.

Up goes the curtain.

Nina is a star—

a pretty good star.

And she is the only one

who **really** shines.